Treasure Island

Treasury of Illustrated Classics

Treasure Island

by
Robert Louis Stevenson

**Abridged, adapted,
and illustrated**
by
quadrum■
Quadrum Solutions, India

Modern Publishing
A Division of Unisystems, Inc.
New York, New York 10022

Cover art by

Contents

Chapter 1

The Old Sea Dog at the Admiral Benbow

I write this story at the tender age of seventeen, because Squire Trelawney, Dr. Livesey, and the rest of these gentlemen have asked me to write everything about Treasure Island, from start to finish.

I think back to the time when my father ran the Admiral Benbow Inn, and of that brown, old seaman with a saber cut, who first took shelter under our roof.

I remember him clearly, walking to the inn door, followed by a man who was pulling along a hand barrow in which he had put his sea chest. He was a tall, strong, and heavy man, his pigtail falling over his dirty, blue coat, his hands rough and scratched with black, broken nails, and a saber cut across one cheek. He looked around the area, and sang that song he would always sing in a high voice,

"Fifteen men on a dead man's chest—
Yo-Ho-Ho and a bottle of rum!"

Then he tapped the door with the stick he carried, until my

father opened it. He asked for a glass of rum, and when he got it, he drank it slowly, as if he was enjoying the taste.

"This is a handy cove," said the seaman to my father "Do you have a lot of visitors?"

"No, not too many," replied my father.

"Well, I like this place!" said the seaman.

He called out to the man pulling the barrow, "Here you, matey! Bring my chest over here. I'll be staying here for a while." He turned to my father. "I'm a very simple man. All I will need is rum and bacon. You may call me Captain. And this is for your services ..." He threw three or four pieces of gold near the door.

There was something strange about our guest. Even though he called himself a captain, he looked like a mere mate, or a skipper who was used to obeying orders. He had asked about the inns along the coast and since our inn was well spoken of, he decided to stay there.

All day, the silent man would stand upon the cliffs, with a brass telescope in his hand; all evening he would sit by the fire, drinking rum. Every day when he came back from the cliffs to the inn, he would ask if any sailors had passed by. At first we thought that he was feeling lonely and wanted to be around people like him, but then we realized that he desperately wanted to avoid them. If any sailor stayed on at the inn for a night, he would observe them through a curtain for a bit before entering the room.

One day he took me aside, and promised to give me a silver penny on the first of every month if I kept

an eye out for a "seafaring man with one leg." The idea of a man with only one leg terrified me! I started having nightmares of him. Sometimes, when the captain

drank a lot, he would either start singing old sea songs, or he would order drinks for everyone and ask them to sing along with him. The house would often echo with,

"Yo-Ho-Ho and a bottle of rum!"

The people only sang because they were afraid of the captain. Whenever he drank too much, he would become very angry if nothing happened his way. He would not allow anyone to leave the inn until he went to bed himself.

What frightened people most were his stories. He would always tell stories about hangings, or walking the plank, or storms at sea. My father always said that the inn would be ruined as people would stop coming there. But I always thought that his presence brought a lot of excitement into the quiet country life here.

In one way, we did think the inn would close down, for he stayed month after month until all the money was gone. If my father asked for more, the captain would just stare at him until he left the room.

The captain never changed his clothing, never spoke to anyone unless it was with the neighbors or when he drank too much. And in all this time, none of us ever knew what was in his sea chest.

One afternoon, Dr. Livesey came to see a patient. I couldn't help noticing the difference between the neat, well-mannered doctor and the rough, dirty pirate. Suddenly the captain started singing,

"Fifteen men on a dead man's chest—
Yo-Ho-Ho and a bottle of rum!
Drink and the devil had
done for the rest—
Yo-Ho-Ho and a
bottle of rum!"

Dr. Livesey looked up angrily at the captain for a moment before he started speaking to his patient. When the captain slammed his palm on the table, everybody in the room became silent, all except Dr. Livesey, who continued to talk with his patient.

The captain shouted out, "Silence there, between decks!"

"Were you talking to me, sir?" asked the doctor, and when he got a 'yes' as a reply, he added, "Sir, if you keep drinking like that, you will die!"

The captain was furious! He took out his knife and tried to pin the doctor with it. But the doctor didn't even move a muscle! He told the captain, "If you don't put away your knife, I will make sure you are hanged!" The doctor added, "I am not only a doctor, but also the magistrate. If I hear any complaints about you, I will see that you are severely punished."

Soon after saying that, the doctor left the inn. For the next few evenings, we saw only good behavior from the captain.

Chapter 2

Black Dog Appears and Disappears

It was a bitter cold winter, with long, hard frosts and heavy gales.

Unfortunately, my poor father wouldn't be alive to see the spring. The inn was left in the hands of my mother and me.

One morning, the captain rose earlier than usual. With the spyglass in his hand he went to the beach, his cutlass swinging beneath his coat. I was laying the breakfast table, when the door opened and a man walked in. He was a pale, thin, and tall person, and had two fingers of his left hand missing. Even though he had a sword, he didn't look like one to fight, and though this man didn't look like a sailor, he had something of the sea about him.

He asked for rum, and called me from where he was sitting. "Is this the table of my mate, Bill?" he asked.

I told him that it was the captain's table.

"Well," he said, "Bill would want to be called captain. He has a cut on his right cheek? Is he around?"

I told him the captain had gone out for a walk.

When we saw the captain approaching, he said "Let's give Bill a little surprise." He hid us both behind the door. He had loosened

his sword and stood ready. When the captain walked in, the man called out, "Bill!"

The captain had the look of a man who had seen a ghost.

"Black Dog!" he gasped.

"And who else?" asked the stranger. "As always, here I am to see you. Ah, it's been a long time since I lost these two fingers ..."

"Well," said the captain. "Now that you've found me, what is it you want?"

Black Dog sent me away.

Suddenly I heard shouting and when I rushed back in, I saw the captain with his sword drawn, chasing Black Dog. Despite bleeding from the shoulder, Black Dog ran quickly, as if his life depended on it. The captain stood at the entrance of the inn and stared at him in utter shock. He ran his hands over his eyes and then suddenly, he fainted! The captain looked as pale as death.

"Call for the doctor!" cried my mother, who came to see what had happened.

When Dr. Livesey examined him, he said that the captain had had a stroke. He sent me for water and then tore open the captain's sleeve. His strong, muscular arm revealed many tattoos, one of them being a man hanging from a noose around his neck. The name "BILLY BONES" was written below it.

"We must try to save this Billy Bones's life," said the doctor. He then cut open a vein and blood started pouring out. The captain woke up and frowned slightly when he saw the doctor. Suddenly he asked nervously, "Where is Black Dog?"

The doctor replied "There is no Black Dog here. You've just had a stroke. I saved your life ... against my will, Mr. Bones..."

"That is not my name," interrupted the captain.

"That is not my interest. I am here to tell you that if you continue to have rum, you will surely die. Good day to you."

The doctor told me that if the captain had another stroke, he would die.

Chapter 3

The Black Spot

By afternoon, I entered the captain's room. He saw me coming in and he barked out, "I can't lie in bed for a week! I've been having visions of old Flint himself! Tell me," he said, "have you seen that sailor?"

I asked him if he meant Black Dog. He shook his head "No not Black Dog. This sailor's much

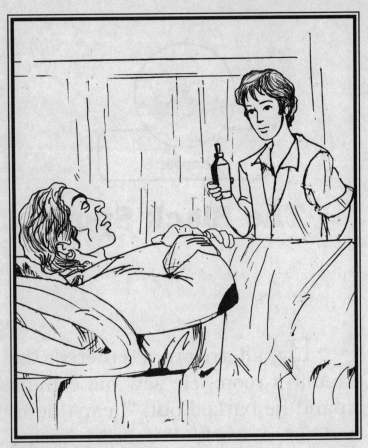

worse. He may give me a death note. We call that note a Black Spot. They're after my sea chest. Now be a good lad and get me a glass of rum."

I refused. "Oh, come now, lad! The doctor himself said I could have a glass once in a while!"

I sighed and got him a glass of rum, which he finished greedily.

"Ah, that's much better," he said, satisfied. "You see, lad, I was Flint's first mate, and am the only one who knows where the treasure is hidden. The man with one leg and Black Dog are after it. You keep an eye out for them and I promise I will share the treasure with you."

I told him all I wanted was the money he owed my father. Unfortunately, that very same night, my dear father died.

The day after the funeral, I was standing by the back door

thinking of my father, when I saw a blind man making his way toward the inn. He was bent over a knobbly, old stick.

When he asked out loud where he was, I answered, "The Admiral Benbow Inn." He asked me to help him inside. As I stretched out my hand toward him, I saw that he was eyeless. Suddenly, he caught my hand in a very strong grip and twisted it behind my back.

"Now boy," he said calmly. "Take me to the captain or I will break your arm. When you are near him, tell him that there is a friend to see him."

I did as I was commanded. The captain, on seeing the blind man, sat up looking frightened

and sick. He tried to rise, but was too weak.

"Now Bill, stay where you are," said the blind man. "We have business to finish. Hold out your left hand. Boy, take his left hand by the wrist and bring it near my right hand." I did as I was told. He dropped something into the captain's hand.

"It is done," he said. Without saying another word, he ran out of the door with amazing speed. The captain looked into his palm with horror, saying, "Ten o'clock! I have six hours left!"

Saying that, he jumped up to his feet. All of a sudden, he went still, grabbed his throat, and fell on the floor. I tried to revive him, but it was too late. The captain was dead. He had had another stroke. Even though I never liked him much, I burst into tears. After all, it was the second death in a row that I had witnessed in two days.

Chapter 4

The Sea Chest

I immediately told my mother everything I knew, and we knew then that we were in quite a tricky situation.

The captain's shipmates would be coming for the chest soon. Each and every sound that we heard filled us with fear. We knew it wouldn't be safe to remain in the house for long, with the pirates coming.

We decided to go to the nearest village for help. We quietly sneaked out into the night. This village was in the opposite direction to that from which the blind man had come.

We were relieved to see the lights on in the village. But when we got there, everyone refused to help us on hearing Captain Flint's name. Many of the villagers had heard about him, and his stories filled them with terror.

All they gave us was a loaded pistol and a promise to lend us horses in case we needed them. They agreed to go and get the doctor's help, but no one wanted to help protect the inn.

My mother cursed the lot. She said angrily, "If none of you dare, Jim and I dare. We will return to the inn and face our problems without the help of you cowardly men. I will not lose the money that belongs to my fatherless boy!"

With heavy hearts, my mother and I made our way back to the inn, with the full moon lighting our path. We quickened our pace, in case we were seen in the moonlight. To our relief, we managed to get back to the inn without any problems.

I bolted the door from the inside. It was just me and my mother alone, along with the dead body of the captain. My mother told me to draw the curtains so that the buccaneers wouldn't be able to see us.

"Now we have to get the key off him. God knows that I can't touch that thing. You do it, Jim, but hurry!" said my mother.

I knelt next to the body and found the crumpled paper the

captain had feared getting. It read "YOU HAVE TILL TEN." Our clock struck six, and we were relieved, we still had four hours left. I searched the pockets for the key, but with no luck.

"It must be around his neck . . . ," said my mother quietly.

I opened his collar and, sure enough, there was the key, tied to a string around his neck. I took it

off him and rushed to his room, my mother following me.

The sea chest looked like any seaman's chest, his having the initial "B" on it. My mother took the key and opened the chest. Inside were clean, unworn clothes, pistols, silver, and trinkets from faraway lands. Beneath these were parchments and a sack of gold.

"We will take only what we were owed," said my mother. "We are honest people." She asked me to hold open an empty bag, and started dropping the coins one by one into it.

Suddenly, I heard a noise and told my mother to stay quiet. From the street I heard the tapping of the blind man's cane and then heard

him pulling at the lock of the door. I heard him retreating when we didn't open.

"Mother," I said, "let's take everything and go!" But she

wouldn't budge. Suddenly we heard a whistle from the street and she quickly changed her mind.

"I'll take what I have! You take those papers!" she exclaimed.

After taking everything, we ran out of the house into the night. We heard voices coming our way. My mother held my hand and said to me, "Take the money. I'm going to faint."

Cursing our bad luck, I caught her in my arms and dragged her under the bridge near the inn. The bridge was too low for us to crawl under, but we managed. We stayed there, my mother mostly visible, hearing voices in the distance.

Chapter 5

The Last of the Blind Man

My curiosity was stronger than my fear. I crept from under the bridge to the edge of the road and watched my enemies emerge from the mist. There were about seven or eight of them. The blind man led them.

"Down with the door!" he ordered as soon as they reached the inn. They broke it down only to be surprised at it being unlocked already. They entered the Admiral Benbow Inn. A moment later, I heard a startled cry. "Bill's dead!"

The blind man swore at their delay. "Search him, you blabbering fools. Find that key!" He told a few of them to go to the captain's room and get the chest. I could hear the footsteps going upstairs. Again, I heard sounds of astonishment. Someone opened the window and called out to the blind man, who was standing on the street, "Pew! Someone's been here before us. Except for the money, everything else has been taken!"

"Forget the money!" he answered. "Where's Flint's map? Is it on his body?"

After getting a negative response, he cursed, "It's that boy and his mother. I wish I had put out his eyes when I'd had the chance. They were here before! They had bolted the door earlier. Find them! They must be close by!"

The men tore apart our inn trying to find us. Just then I heard the same whistle that put fear into me and my mother earlier.

"That's Dirk," said one man, "Time for us to leave now!"

Pew lashed out at them, calling Dirk a coward and all of them fools for not searching harder. "Find it! We'll be rich! You were all too scared to face Bill, but not me, and I'm blind!"

With that, he began striking the men with his cane, causing uproar amongst them. They started fighting like cats and dogs. The sound of hooves and a pistol

Officer Dance and his men. The officers took off in search of the other men who had accompanied the blind man. When they arrived at the docks, they saw a small boat that had been cut loose, floating away with these escaping men. The officers then helped to take my mother to the inn, where she was revived.

The inn was a wreck. Everything was destroyed. After telling the officers my story, we concluded that the parchment scrolls in my pocket were what those men were after. We decided to go over to Dr. Livesey's and give him the parchments for safekeeping. The officers helped me onto a horse and I was on my way.

shot broke them apart. The buccaneers ran in every direction, except for old Pew. He was left crying and cursing out their names as he rushed past me. But when he heard the sound of horses, he panicked and ran. He lost his footing and fell right under the hooves of the horses. The horses trampled him to death.

Breathing heavily, I looked up at the riders. It was Chief

Chapter 6

The Captain's Papers

We rode to Dr. Livesey's with the chief officer, Mr. Dance, leading the way. We knocked on the door, which was opened by a maid.

"Is Dr. Livesey around?" asked Mr. Dance.

"No, sir," said the maid. "He left in the evening to have dinner with the squire."

"We will go to the squire's house," ordered Mr. Dance.

At the squire's house, a servant led us down a passage to a grand library. The squire and Dr. Livesey

were sitting by the fire, each with a pipe in one hand.

This was the first time I had seen the squire closely. He was over six feet tall, broad in proportion, with a rough, ruddy face, reddened and lined because of his long travels.

He quickly asked us the purpose of our visit, and after they heard us, Mr. Trelawney, the squire, got up and paced the floor.

"Mr. Dance," Dr. Livesey began, "you are a very noble fellow. I will consider your putting an end to the blind man as doing a good deed. This boy Jim here is as good as gold, too."

The doctor asked if I had the parchment scrolls with me. He took the oilskin packet into which I had placed them, and put it in his pocket.

Suddenly, the doctor asked the squire if he'd heard of a man called Flint.

"Heard of him! He is the most bloodthirsty buccaneer who ever sailed. All pirates fear him."

"Tell me," said the doctor, "If what I have in my pocket is some sort of clue to Flint's treasure, will that treasure be worth a lot?"

"Yes," replied the squire. "Very well! Now if Jim agrees, we will open the packet," said the doctor.

When the packet was opened, it contained two things: a book and a sealed paper. The doctor and I were puzzled by the strange markings and figures in columns in the book. The squire immediately understood what they were.

"That is the rascal's account book!" So it was. We turned our

attention to the sealed packet. The doctor opened it carefully. A map fell out with notes and directions. Just past a hill marked "the Spyglass" was a note written in a handwriting different from that in the book, which said, "Bulk of treasure here." The back of the note had a few more directions, leading to a place called Skeleton Island.

"Livesey," said the squire, "you will give up your practice at once. I will go to Bristol first thing tomorrow. In ten days, I will get us the best ship and the best crew ever. Jim can come as a cabin boy. I'll be the admiral, you; the ship's doctor. We'll take Redruth, Joyce, and Hunter."

"The one man I am afraid of is you, Trelawney, for you cannot keep a secret!" said the doctor. "There are pirates out there who will kill for this map, who will take any risk to get what we have with us. We must stay together until we are at sea. I'll stay with Jim, but none of us must speak a word about this to anyone." The squire promised to be silent.

Chapter 7

The Sea Cook

Our preparations took longer than we expected. While the doctor and the squire attended to their own businesses, I stayed at the hall, under the watch of Tom Redruth, the gamekeeper.

I spent hours studying the map, imagining how our adventure would be. But nothing I imagined was as strange and tragic as what happened when our journey began.

One day, a letter arrived addressed to the doctor, but with instructions to have it read by Tom Redruth or me if the doctor was unavailable. Since Redruth couldn't read very well, I read it out loud.

It was a letter from the squire, stating that he had found a ship called the *Hispaniola*. He even

came across an old sailor, who offered to be the ship's cook and could help to get a crew together. His name was Long John Silver. He had lost a leg in the service of his country. Long John Silver not only assembled the crew, he also picked out the first mate, Mr. Arrow. The letter ended with the squire asking the doctor, myself, and Redruth to meet him in Bristol as soon as possible. He also added that I may spend one night with my mother before we left.

When I got back to the inn, I was happy to see my mother in good health. The squire had gotten the entire inn rebuilt and painted. The squire also sent my mother a young boy as an apprentice to help

out in my absence. On seeing the boy, I realized that he had taken my place next to my mother, and that I was truly leaving home for a long time. This thought brought tears to my eyes.

I left the next morning and soon, the Admiral Benbow Inn was out of sight. We travelled to Bristol by train. The moment we stepped off, we headed toward the inn, where the squire was waiting for us. On our way there, I saw many ships. Though I had lived by the seaside all my life, I seemed never to have been so close to the sea itself.

I was imagining my life as a sailor, when the squire suddenly appeared before me. He was dressed like a ship's admiral, in all his finery.

"Oh, sir," I cried, "when do we set sail?"

"Sail?" he answered. "We sail tomorrow!"

Chapter 8

At the Sign of
the Spyglass

After breakfast, the squire gave me a note to be delivered to Long John Silver. He also gave me directions on how to get to the tavern, where I could find him. I made my way through the crowded docks until I found the tavern. It had the sign of a spyglass on it.

It was quite a neat, little tavern and it was full of sailors talking loudly.

I saw the cook come out of a room, and I simply knew at first glance that he was Long John Silver. His left leg was cut off from the knee; he carried a crutch, hopping on it with great speed! He was tall and very strong, and had a big, pale face, but he looked intelligent and was smiling. He spoke and laughed with the men there.

When I first had been told that he was a one-legged man, I immediately thought that he was the sailor that the dead captain had asked me to look out for. However, looking at him, I knew he was not the one.

I took a deep breath and walked up to him. "Mr. Silver, sir?" I asked, holding out the note.

"Yes, my lad," he said, smiling at me, "that is my name. And who might you be?" He read the squire's note, and his smile broadened. He took my hand and shook it firmly.

"So you are our new cabin boy! I am pleased to meet you!"

Just then, one of the customers got up and rushed out of the door. But I recognized him from his missing two fingers on his hand and the expression on his face when he saw me.

"Oh," I cried, "stop him. That's Black Dog!"

"I don't care who he is— he hasn't paid for his drink!" cried Long John. He sent one of his men after him. He asked me to repeat the name again. I told him that he was one of the buccaneers.

"So?" he cried. "He was here? In my house!" He looked at a man sitting alone on a table. "Morgan!" he called out. "You were drinking

with him, weren't you? Come here and tell us what he told you."

A gray-haired, red-faced sailor called Morgan came forward. He told Long John Silver that this was the first time he had seen Black Dog. He had never met him before. After finding out that the conversation was more or less general, Long John Silver sent Morgan back to his table. He told me that he had seen Black Dog come in with a blind beggar often.

"Pew! The blind man, his name's Pew!" I told him.

"So it is! Did he talk of throwing you overboard? It's him I'll throw overboard if I get the chance!"

I started to grow quite suspicious, seeing Black Dog here, and I observed Long John Silver. He was quite good at convincing me that he would have gone after

Black Dog himself, had he had both his legs. We decided to tell Squire Trelawney about this. On our way there, he told me about the different ships we passed by and told me old sea stories. He kept explaining nautical terms to me until I understood them perfectly. I saw then that he was the best possible sailor.

When we arrived at the inn, we found Dr. Livesey there along with the squire. Long John told them what had happened at the tavern, not missing a single detail. He even asked for my confirmation on the event. The squire and the doctor regretted that Black Dog had managed to get away. After congratulating Long John, we all agreed to meet aboard the ship at four o'clock that afternoon.

"Well, Trelawney," said the doctor, "you were right about Long John Silver. He will prove to be very worthy to us. That man is an ace!"

He turned to me. "Now, Jim, let us go see our ship!"

Chapter 9

Powder and Arms

We quickly made our way to the harbor. Our ship, the *Hispaniola,* was docked beside other great ships. We were introduced to Mr. Arrow, the ship's mate, a dark man with studs in his ears, and squint eyes. Soon after, we met the captain, Captain

Smollett, who asked to speak to the squire as soon as possible.

"Ah, Captain!" said Trelawney. "What have you to say? All's well, I hope."

"Well, sir," began Captain Smollett, "I'll be quite honest with you. I don't like the men, and I don't like my officer."

"What about the ship?" asked Trelawney.

The captain said he had no complaints about the ship. He felt that the men already knew too much about the mission to find the treasure. He didn't think it was right that he, being captain, knew much less than they did about the journey.

"I don't like treasure voyages. I especially don't like them when they are not secret voyages, voyages that even the cook's parrot knows of! If I may say so, what you gentlemen are about to embark on is very dangerous."

He asked us if we were absolutely sure and determined to take this journey.

"Yes," the squire answered.

"Very well," said the captain, "as you've patiently heard me saying useless things to you, allow me to add a few more words. I would suggest that you separate the powder from the arms. Also, that all of your own men sleep together in the same cabin."

"Any more?" asked the squire.

"One more," said the captain. "There is to be no more mentioning of the treasure. The men already know the exact location of the island!"

The squire protested by saying that he had told no one about the location, and we believed him. But the captain proved him wrong by describing the map and the exact latitudes and longitudes of the location of the treasure. The doctor then understood the captain's concerns. The captain feared unrest amongst the crew members. The doctor reassured him.

"You are very understanding, sir," said the captain. "When I came in here, I thought I was going to be discharged. I knew the squire wouldn't listen to me."

The squire angrily told the captain, "You are right about that! Had the doctor not been here, I would have sent you packing. I have heard all that you have to say and I will do as you want. That does not mean I think any better of you!"

The captain only bowed and left, totally unaffected. When we got onto the ship, the men were already taking out the powder and arms, yo-ho-ho-ing at their efforts. Mr. Arrow was supervising them. I quite liked my new sleeping arrangement. When Long John Silver arrived shortly, he tried to protest our changes.

"These are my orders," said the captain to Long John. "You may go down and cook supper for the crew."

Long John nodded his agreement, saluted the captain, and went to belowdecks.

"That's a good man," said the doctor.

It was clear that the captain would be quite strict. He even sent me belowdecks with a sharp word to help Long John Silver. As I hurried off, I heard him telling the doctor loudly, "I'll have no favorites on my ship."

At that moment, I started sharing the squire's dislike for Captain Smollett.

Chapter 10

The Apple Barrel

We worked all night—I had never been so tired. But I still kept awake, for each moment on the *Hispaniola* was new and exciting for me. While the men worked, Long John Silver, whom everyone called Barbecue, took up his crutch and at once began to sing the words I knew so well:

"Fifteen men on a dead man's chest..."
And the crew joined in with,

"Yo-Ho-Ho and a bottle of rum!"

Just before dawn, the *Hispaniola* began her voyage to Treasure Island. She proved to be a wonderful vessel.

Mr. Arrow turned out to be much worse than the captain

thought. He was always drunk and seasick.

One day, it so happened that he disappeared over the railing completely.

The captain now had to find a new mate. He took Israel Hands, a cunning-looking old seaman who was also a good friend of Long John Silver.

In his own way, Long John turned out to be a great seaman. He was very helpful, and the men loved him. His parrot was named Captain Flint, after the famous pirate.

The captain and the squire, however, remained distant with each other. The squire didn't hide his displeasure toward the captain.

The crew, however, was quite content. There was plenty of good wine and food and even a big barrel of apples on deck.

Once, after sundown, I decided to go and get myself one juicy apple. The barrel was nearly empty, so I had to climb into the barrel to get one of the last few

apples. Once there, I sat down and felt quite sleepy.

I must have dozed off, for I woke up hearing muffled voices. I felt a body leaning against the barrel. I heard a voice and recognized it to be Long John Silver's. I had only heard the first few words when I trembled with fear. For what I heard after that made me realize that the lives of the few honest men left onboard depended on me alone.

"The famous pirate Flint was captain of the ship called *Walrus* and I was quartermaster," said Long John Silver. "It was on that voyage that I lost my leg and Pew lost his eyesight. There was so much gold on the ship that

the crew was drawing blood from one another."

I soon realized that he was just telling lies to the youngest worker on the deck.

It was clear that the boy was influenced by Long John Silver, who continued to flatter and impress him with his tales. I realized that "Gentlemen of

Fortune" meant pirates, and that he was one of them. Just then, Israel Hands came up to speak to John.

"I want to know one thing," said Israel. "How long are we going to stand off? I've had enough of Captain Smollett! I want to enter his cabin and kill him."

Long John Silver turned angrily at him. "You will kill the captain who is steering this blessed ship for us? The man who will lead us to the treasure! Are you out of your mind? You will do no such thing! You'll wait and act on my signal only!

But make sure you leave Smollett to me," Long John continued. "I would very much like to wring that calf's head off with my bare hands."

He turned to the lad, Dick, and told him to get an apple from the barrel. You can imagine my shock and terror as I sat in the barrel. Luckily, Israel unknowingly saved my life by saying that the thought of mutiny made him too excited to eat. They all decided to get themselves mugs of rum and went belowdecks.

Suddenly, at that moment, the moon rose up and a shout rang out all over the ship;

"Land ho!"

Chapter 11

Council of War

Everyone started running onto the deck to see the land. The crew gathered at the stern of the ship, including Dr. Livesey and myself. The fog had lifted, and in the moonlight we saw in the distance two low hills, about a couple of miles apart. Rising behind one of them was a third and higher hill, whose peak was still buried in the fog.

I could hear Captain Smollett giving orders for the ship to dock. He then turned toward us and asked if any one of us had been to this land before.

"Yes, sir," replied Long John Silver. "I came here when I worked as a cook with a trader. This island is called Skeleton Island, a place where pirates lived."

He also explained that the big hill, whose peak was still buried in the fog, was called the Spyglass. This was because this hill was used as a lookout by the pirates when they had to unload the loot from the ships.

On hearing this, the captain asked Long John to identify whether this was the same place as shown in the map. Long John was disappointed that the map was not the one that belonged to the dead captain but a freshly drawn map. He confirmed that this was the same place, and told the captain to drop the anchor.

The captain then ordered Long John to go down belowdecks. As Long John passed by me, he laid a hand on my shoulder, telling me that I would enjoy this island. I shuddered—I was scared of his cruelty, duplicity, and power ever since I had overheard his cunning conversation.

Captain Smollett, the squire, and Dr. Livesey were talking together on the quarterdeck. I was longing to tell them what I had overheard from inside the apple barrel; however, I didn't want to disturb them. Just then, the doctor called me to his side.

As soon as I was near enough to speak and not be overheard, I said, "Doctor, let me speak. Get the captain and the squire down to the cabin, and then make some pretence to send for me. I have terrible news."

The doctor's face showed no worry as he turned toward the squire and the captain. They spoke for a while, and though no one gave any signs of concern, I knew that the doctor had given them my message.

The captain called all his crew on the deck and told them that the place they had been sailing to had been reached. He praised them for the wonderful job they had done to reach there, and informed them that the squire, the doctor, and he were going down to drink to everyone's health. The crew cheered after him. The cheer was so full and hearty that it was difficult to believe that these very men were after our blood.

Soon afterward, they called for me. When I went down, I found all three seated around the table, a bottle of Spanish wine and some

raisins before them. The doctor was smoking away, with his wig on his lap, and I knew he was upset. The stern window was open, for it was a warm night, and you could see the moon shining behind.

"Now, Hawkins," said the squire, "you have something to say. Speak up."

I told them what I had overheard in the apple barrel. Nobody interrupted me till I was done. They were still, but they kept their eyes upon my face from the beginning till the end. The doctor asked me to sit down. They offered me wine and raisins and cheered me for my courage and good work.

The squire and the captain realized their mistake in taking

Long John Silver for this mission and allowing him to select the crew. They were shocked that the crew they were trusting actually wanted to harm them for the treasure.

The captain then chalked out a plan. His plan had three steps. He said, "Firstly, we must go on, because we can't turn back. If I order the crew to leave now, they will rise to fight. Secondly, we have time before we get to the treasure. Thirdly, there are some crew members who can be trusted. We will plan our move when they are least expecting it."

They identified the trustworthy crew to be the squire's three servants, myself, the doctor, the squire, and the captain himself. I was given the responsibility to keep a lookout for any odd happenings, and to keep my ears open for any further news.

I began to feel pretty desperate and helpless; and yet, it was indeed through me that safety came. However, the truth was that there were only seven out of the twenty-six on whom we knew we could rely; and out of these seven one was a boy.

Chapter 12

My Shore Adventure

The island looked different when I came on deck the next day. The surface was covered with gray woods. The hill ran upward, past the vegetation, in spires of moss-clear rocks. They were all shaped funnily, and the one shaped like a spyglass, at least 400 feet high,

was by far the largest and strangest formation on the island.

As we neared the cove we didn't hear a single sound, except for the waves crashing. All of us who had met last night were worried about Long John. We decided to meet in the cabin once more.

"If I give another order," said the captain, "there will be mutiny. If I don't, Long John will know that I am holding back because I know what he is up to."

"Well," asked the squire, "what can we do?"

The captain went on deck and announced the outing.

"Whoever would like to, may go ashore. I will fire a gun half an hour before sundown. That is when you must return to the ship."

With that, the men jumped up, for they were eager to find the treasure.

In the end, thirteen men went ashore and six stayed aboard. I decided to hide myself in one of the boats, but unfortunately,

Long John saw me. At that moment, I regretted my actions. The moment my boat landed, I jumped off and ran into the woods. I ran and ran until I could do so no longer. I could hear Long John calling out my name.

I was so happy to have given Long John Silver the slip that I began to enjoy exploring the island. I came across some marshy land full of swaying willows and odd-shaped trees that rose from the swamps. There was a sandy stretch that went on for about half a mile, lined with pine trees. On the far side of the hill stood one of the hills with its jagged peak shining brightly in the sun.

The crew was far behind me. I went into the forest to look around. I managed to see a rattle snake coming out from a rock, with its head raised and fangs open. I saw huge tortoises and magical flowering plants that you can only imagine.

Suddenly, I heard a rustle among the bushes. I figured my shipmates must be close. So I ran, crouched behind the nearest tree, and quietly waited. I heard voices, one of whose was Long John Silver's. I inched closer to catch their conversation.

"Mate," he was saying, "you are more valuable than gold to me, that's why I'm warning you now. You can't change the plan. Save yourself by joining in. Tell me, what could they do to me if they found out that I was talking to you right now?"

"Silver," said the sailor, "you may have let yourself be led away, but not me."

He turned his back on Long John Silver and marched away,

but he was not destined to go far.
Long John leaned back, aimed his
crutch, and lanced it toward the
unfortunate man. Its point hit the
center of Tom's back, and he fell
down with a cry. He was given no

time to recover, for Long John, quick as a monkey, was on top of him with his knife out. He stabbed him twice, right up to the hilt, killing him.

I managed not to faint as I watched Long John Silver wipe off the blood, panting at the same time. He then took out a whistle from his pocket and blew it twice. I knew he had called out for

the others. If they had killed two honest men, would they not kill me, too?

I began to crawl back, and as I did, I heard a chorus of voices. I turned and ran through the thicket. I didn't know how I would be able to get back to the ship. I knew that if I was caught, the men would wring my neck.

I said my good-byes silently to the *Hispaniola*, to the doctor, to the squire, and to the captain. There was nothing left for me except death by starvation, or death at the hands of the mutineers. I ran until I reached the foot of a little hill. My heart pounding, a fresh wave of fear brought me to a standstill.

Chapter 13

The Man of
the Island

I saw a figure leap with great speed behind the trunk of a pine tree. I could not tell whether it was a man, or a monkey. It was dark and shaggy. I started running away, but that creature started chasing me. I was more afraid of it

than I had been of Long John Silver, but I remembered that I had a loaded pistol with me. I stopped and turned around to face the creature. He stopped running and started walking toward me.

It was a man. I asked him who he was.

"Ben Gunn," he answered, his voice rusty from lack of use. "I haven't spoken to anyone in more than three years!"

He was sunburned and bearded. His lips were cracked, and his clothes were nothing more than pieces of an old ship's canvas tied together. I asked if he had been shipwrecked. He said that he had been marooned. I knew what that word meant. It was a severe punishment for any sailor, where someone accused of a terrible act is left all alone on an island.

He went on to tell me that he would make me a rich man, and

quickly asked if the ship belonged to Flint.

Somehow, I trusted the man. I told him that the ship did not belong to Flint, and that he was dead, and also that some of his men were murderers and mutineers.

"Are you talking in particular about a man with one leg?" he gasped.

I nodded in agreement, seeing him shiver and turn pale. I told him all that had taken place so far. He asked me if the squire would take him on, and give him a thousand pounds if he helped. I said that he would.

This is what he revealed to me: "I was onboard with Flint's men when Flint had gone ashore with six men and buried the treasure. He killed all six of them, and he never told a soul where the treasure was kept. Those who asked were told that they were welcome to stay on the island and find the treasure. They all refused, of course. Three years later, I was on another ship and when I saw the island, I told the crew that I would find the treasure. After three days of searching and not finding it, they cursed me and left me here with only a musket, a spade, and a shovel."

He added that I should tell the squire that when not pining for cheese and home, Ben had been occupied with another matter that would interest him.

I told him there was no way to get back to the ship. "Well," said Ben, pointing to a cove, "we can always use that boat that I've built. I keep it by a white rock that lies farther down toward the shore."

Suddenly we heard cannon fire and gunshots ringing through the air. I knew that there was a fight onboard the ship.

Chapter 14

How the Ship Was Abandoned

*Narrative as added
by Dr. Livesey*

That afternoon, when the two boats went ashore, the captain, the squire, and I started talking, at the same time keeping an eye on the six men who were left onboard, sitting and sulking. Hunter came a moment later and told us that Jim had gone ashore. We were disheartened instantly.

It was decided that Hunter and I should go ashore and find out more. We went directly for the stockade, which was marked on the map. It was a sturdy, well-protected place with a fresh-water spring and a high fence, perfect for

defense. We soon heard the cry of a man being killed, and we immediately thought it was poor Jim Hawkins.

We rowed back to the ship and found the squire and one of his men looking very pale. We put Redruth in the galley with loaded guns to stand guard. Hunter brought the jolly boat around, while Joyce and I loaded it with gunpowder, weapons, biscuits, pork, and my medicine chest. On the deck, the captain had a gun pointed to the crew. He was saying, "Mr. Hands, we will shoot the first man who moves."

The shocked men ran belowdecks to find Redruth armed and ready. They came back up

again and skidded to a halt upon seeing the captain's guns. We had already made it to the shore by then. We left Joyce to guard the stockade while we quickly unloaded our things. We then rowed back to the ship, thoroughly exhausted. Once there we loaded the jolly boats with more cargo and

got ready to row back to shore once more.

But first, we took all the guns that we could and dumped them overboard. Hearing voices from the shore made us realize that our time was up. Before loading everything into the jolly boat, the captain called down to the men belowdecks, "Abraham Gray, I am speaking to you. I order you to follow your captain. You are different from the rest. I give you thirty seconds to join me. Hurry! I risk my life and the lives of my friends here."

The moment he finished saying this, we heard a scuffle and Gray appeared with a knife cut on his face. We got into our jolly boats and headed out.

Chapter 15

The Fight

*Narrative as added
by Dr. Livesey*

Our trip this time was slower. The jolly boat was overloaded with men and cargo. Also, the tide was flowing against us; it kept pushing us back into the sea. Suddenly, the captain cried out, "The cannon!" Only then did we realize that the

weapons were laid out on the deck. We saw a few pirates on deck, aiming the guns our way.

Gray told us that Israel Hands was Flint's gunner. We knew then that we were being aimed at by an expert. Among us, the squire was the best with a rifle. He stood up and fired at the *Hispaniola*. Israel ducked, and the man behind him was shot instead.

The cannon was reloaded quickly. As the squire pulled the trigger once more, they let loose their shot as well. The bullets went whizzing past our heads. The jolly boat shook because of the disturbance in the water, caused by the shower of pellets. Its front part went underwater.

The squire and I managed to keep our guns above the water as we stood in shallow surf. Everyone else jumped into the water with our cargo. Their guns were ruined, leaving only ours to use. We also found that all our provisions were gone. To add to our troubles, we heard voices coming near us, and feared being cut off from getting to the stockade.

We ran quickly to the stockade and with each step that we took, the buccaneers sounded closer. "Captain," I said, "the squire has the best aim. Give him your gun. His own is useless."

The captain passed his best gun to the squire, who took aim. I, in turn, gave my sword to Gray. We knew he was on our side. We neared the stockade when some of

the mutineers appeared. They saw
us and stopped suddenly. The
squire and I fired, just as Hunter
and Joyce did from the stockade.
One fell dead, shot through the
heart; the rest ran away. Our
victory was short, for someone shot

Redruth. He fell to the ground, not dead, but bleeding. We carried him back to the stockade, where he passed away.

The squire went to the roof of the stockade and tied the flag of England to the top of a fallen tree. He came back and asked me how many weeks it would be till another ship would come to look for us. I told him quite honestly that it could take months. That's when the captain told us that our rations were quite scarce.

Just then, we heard the cannon fire again and heard the ball fall somewhere close to the stockade. We knew they were aiming at us, but we weren't scared.

"Oho!" cried the captain, "Fire away! You'll never hit us from where you are. You will, however, do us a huge favor of finishing off your powder supply!"

That very night, Joyce and Hunter volunteered to try to rescue the supply from the shallow water, where the low tide had left it on the sand. But, unfortunately, Long John's men were already carrying most of it away.

The captain recorded our details in his logbook.

Even as he was finishing, we heard a happy shout.

"Doctor! Squire! Captain! Hullo, Hunter, is that you?" came the cries.

I ran out just in time to see young Jim Hawkins safe and sound, climbing over the stockade wall.

Chapter 16

The Garrison in the Stockade

Narrative resumed by Jim Hawkins

As soon as Ben Gunn saw the Union Jack, he stopped and told me that I would find my friends at the stockade. He assured me that pirates would not fly the British flag, but their own Jolly Roger—the famous black flag with its skull and crossbones in white.

He also told me, that the stockade was built by none other than Flint himself, who was afraid of no one except Long John Silver. "Well, let's go there before Long John himself finds us!" I told him. Ben made me swear that the next day I would send someone from

our camp to meet him, as he had a proposal for us.

"Carry a white handkerchief with you, just to be on the safe side." he warned me. "If you run into Long John Silver, don't let him know that I am on this island. That would ruin everything for us!"

I promised I wouldn't, and at that moment a cannonball went whizzing through the air, sending us both running in opposite directions. I came to a clearing and saw the *Hispaniola* flying the Jolly Roger flag.

I made my way to the stockade. On my way there, I found the white rock where Ben had been hiding his boat. Keeping this in my mind, I made my way over to the fence and into the arms of my friends.

I told them my story and took stock of the log house. It was smoky from our fire, not to mention Gray lying wrapped in a bandage on account of his knife cut, and poor Tom cold and dead under a flag in the corner of the room. The captain wisely kept us busy with chores to do, collecting firewood and digging a grave for Redruth. I told the doctor about Ben.

Even though the captain grumbled, he knew that losing that ship would prove best for us. I was so tired, I slept like a log.

I woke up in the morning to someone shouting, "Flag of truce! It's from Long John Silver himself!"

Chapter 17

Silver's Embassy and the Attack

There were two men outside the stockade, one of them being Long John Silver, waving a white flag.

"Who goes there?" asked Captain Smollett.

"Captain Silver, and this is a flag of truce," came the reply, "I would like to come aboard and make terms."

He hopped his way over the fence and slowly, painfully, made his way up the hill toward us. Once inside, the captain refused to let him inside the fort, so Long John Silver had to sit on the sand across from the captain.

"It is quite cold to be sitting in the sand outside, sir," said Long John Silver.

"That's not my fault," replied the captain. "This is all your doing. You're either the ship's cook or you're Captain Silver, in which case you are a pirate and a mutineer. Therefore, you must hang!"

Long John Silver greeted each one of us when he saw us guarding a point of the fort.

"Well," said Long John Silver, "here it is. We want the treasure, you want your lives. You have a map, and we want it. Now, I mean no harm ..."

With that, the captain burst out in anger and told Long John that he knew his plan. They quietly stared at each other for a long time.

After a while, Long John Silver spoke. "Now, you give us the map and you have a choice. We'll take you back with us and drop you somewhere safe, or, you can stay here and we'll give you half of the treasure. I think that's a fair enough deal."

"Is that all?" asked the captain. "If so, here is my offer. If you come up one by one and unarmed, I shall put cuffs on each of you and take you back to a fair trial. If not, I'll see you all in Davy Jones's locker, drowned dead at the bottom of the sea. No treasure there. You can't sail a ship. These are the last good words you'll have from me. Next will be a bullet in your back. Now get out."

"At least shake hands on it!" cried Long John Silver.

We each refused in turn. With that, Long John Silver got up, spitting in our fresh-water spring as he passed it, and made his way to the fence, where his man dragged him over the side.

As soon as he left, the captain scolded us for having left our posts. Except Gray, who had stayed on. We were ashamed. We then loaded our guns and waited for what would happen next.

"I don't have to tell you what's coming," said the captain. "We're outnumbered. But we can fight if we hold our discipline."

We took our positions. Just then, Joyce asked if he was to shoot if he saw a man.

"Of course!" shouted the captain, and he sat down, fuming. Without wasting any time, Joyce

ran into the woods. His shot was returned by three smoking rounds of fire. When asked if he hit the man, Joyce said he had not.

From that moment, we saw that the attack was on. A group of pirates ran out of the woods and straight to our fence. They climbed over it like monkeys, and we all fired. Three of them fell; one nimbly got up and disappeared. Four others made the fence, while

seven or eight continued to fire toward us with little effect.

Soon, though, four pirates fell on us fiercely and the position was reversed. We had gone from having secure cover to being openly exposed. There were shots everywhere. Captain Smollett alled for us to draw our swords and fight hand-to-hand in the smoke.

On grabbing my sword, I cut my knuckles. I saw Hunter being smashed with his own gun, which was taken by a pirate. I saw the captain slash a mutineer across his face and I heard him yelling in an injured voice.

I turned to find Anderson, the pirate, coming for me, his sword high above his head. I had no time to be afraid, for I lost my footing and fell headfirst, downhill.

When I landed, I groggily saw one pirate coming over the fence with a dagger in his mouth. And then suddenly, the fight was over!

Gray had speared one, and another had been shot as he tried to enter the house. The doctor had cut down the third; the fourth was now turning tail and climbing over the fence.

"Fire—fire from the house!" cried the doctor. "And you, boys, back into cover."

I saw the price we had paid for this victory. Hunter was lying down, stunned. Joyce was killed, shot in the head. The squire was holding a very pale Captain Smollett.

"He's wounded!"

"How many did we take down?" asked the captain.

"Five," the doctor said.

The captain was grimly satisfied with this.

Chapter 18

How My Sea Adventure Began

The mutineers did not return that day. At our end however, Hunter didn't recover from his injuries. He died that very night. The captain was wounded badly.

Just after noon, after seeing that the coast was clear, the doctor took his pistols and headed out to meet Ben. Gray thought him insane for doing so. I couldn't sit and wait, so I sneaked out, filled my pockets with biscuits, and went on my own mission. I wanted to see if Ben's boat was still there and in good condition. I took pistols and powder. I know, it was foolish of me to go alone. But by doing so, I managed to save us all.

I saw Long John Silver and the pirates pulling back to shore from the boat. I could hear his parrot squawking in the wind. When I realized that they were heading in my direction, I hurried to the White Rock. The boat was hidden below it. It was very simple and very light.

I waited until the darkness and fog set in, and I carried the little boat out into the water. From where I was, I could see two lights, one coming from the defeated pirates onshore, the other from the ship. And that was where I quietly and carefully made my way.

The tiny vessel I was in took me to the *Hispaniola* quicker than

I expected. It took a little while to get used to the boat, but it was fairly solid and light on the waters. Soon, I was at the side of the ship.

I reached out and held the thick rope attached to the anchor, called the hawser. It was tight and taut. One cut with my knife, the ship would go humming along the tide. I also knew that the hawser could kill me with the force at which it would snap, if I was not careful. The moment I finished cutting the final threads, it slipped under the water.

There were loud, angry noises coming from the deck. It was Israel Hands and the man who came after me with his knife in his mouth. I heard them call each other terrible names. At that moment, a strong breeze came and

the ship began moving away. Luckily my boat didn't smash itself against the ship. I stood up and saw the two men fighting, holding each other by their throats. I ducked quickly and shut my eyes.

Suddenly, I felt the boat moving quicker. We had gone past the shore! The campfire was right behind me. The ship was moving sideways. The sailors had ceased fighting as they knew something was wrong.

I flattened myself against the bottom of my boat and trembled with fear. I must've been like that for hours. Soon I grew drowsy with the movements of the boat. I fell asleep, dreaming of my home and the Admiral Benbow Inn.

Chapter 19

How I Struck the Jolly Roger

When I woke up, my boat was making its way to the south end of the island, and I was being tossed back and forth by giant waves. I realized that I could either drown or get smashed against sharp rocks, as I didn't have a paddle. The shore was impossible to get to. The boat stopped tossing and it began to go smoothly over the waves. I thought if this continued, I could just about reach land. The sun was burning brightly, and my throat was parched.

As I turned around the next cove, I saw something unbelievable. The *Hispaniola* was heading right at me in full sail! My first thought was that the sailors were chasing me. But then I saw that the ship was moving on its own. There was no one steering it! It occurred to me that I could try to take the ship back to the captain.

But if the pirates were still onboard, could I subdue them all and take control of the ship? The idea was appealing enough.

The wind stopped for just a minute, as did the ship. Then, as suddenly as she stopped, she began to spin toward me with her cabin window open. I saw that the wooden beam that jutted out from the mast would be over my head. Once it was over my head, I jumped up and caught the beam. The ship suddenly rose up in the waves and came crashing down on my little boat.

I held on tightly to the beam as I could easily get tossed back out into the sea. I slowly crawled my way to the deck. What a mess the deck was! The sails were up, but I saw the two watchmen

lying in a heap not far from me.
I saw Israel Hands and the other
man, too. He moved a bit, but
the other man was dead. Just
then, Israel started moaning and

moving about. I saw that he was hurt and bleeding as well. I walked over to him and stood over his body.

He rolled over and called for something to drink. I searched for food and water, and I took these on the deck and gave Israel some of it, but not before having my full share. He groaned and said, "Long John's dead now. Where the heck did you come from?"

"I've come to take back the ship, and you may call me Captain until further notice." He looked at me sourly but didn't say a word. I told him that I would now take down the Jolly Roger. I happily scampered up and cut the flag loose.

"That's the end of Long John Silver," I said. "Well, now," said Hands, "this man and I were going to sail the ship back. But he's dead now, so it's up to us. Why don't you get me

something to tie my bleeding leg with so that I can help you steer the ship?"

"Do you think I'm stupid? I am not going to let you sail back to where Silver is."

I said, "The north is where we shall go."

"I don't have a choice now, do I? I'll sail wherever you want to go. It is your ship and you are Captain after all!" cried Hands.

After that, I helped tie his wound and gave him something to eat. We then sailed back to shore. I noticed that his sad look had turned into a sneer, and that he was watching my every move carefully.

Chapter 20

Back to the Shore with the *Hispaniola*

Under Hands's guidance, we steered the *Hispaniola* over the ocean waves. We soon stopped for a quick meal.

"Captain," he began, "I wonder if you could go belowdecks and get me my glasses. These old eyes

159

could use a little help." I knew he was up to something and wanted me off deck. "Of course. Give me but a moment," I replied.

With that, I ran belowdecks but came back out another way, just behind him. I had taken off my shoes. I saw him carefully look around. Once he was sure he was alone, he gingerly got up and, plucking the bloodied knife from the other man's chest, he tidied it and hid it in his sleeve. It was clear he meant to kill me.

I gave him the spyglass. He told me to follow his orders, calling me Captain Hawkins. He pointed out where we might come in, so I ran about setting sails and making sure we hit our mark.

"Steady, steady now!" said Hands, and at the last moment I turned the ship hard and we made for shore. I was so caught up with work that I didn't realize he was standing behind me until the last minute. I turned and saw him lunging at me. I quickly let go of the sail and it snapped quickly, stopping him dead in his tracks. I ran before he could recover, but he was determined to get me.

I reached for one of my guns and pulled the trigger, only to find that the seawater had made it completely useless. I threw down the gun and ran again, cursing my mistake. For someone who was wounded, he moved quickly! We dodged each other for a bit.

Suddenly, the ship hit the beach, and the jolt threw us both in the air. Luckily, Hands couldn't

get up, so I made my way up the mast. There, I quickly positioned my guns and made them ready. He looked up and sneered. He came toward me, knife between his teeth, and began a slow and painful climb up the mast.

"One more step, Mr. Hands, and I'll blow your brains out!" I said. I even laughed a bit, encouraging myself. He stopped and took the dagger from his mouth to speak. "Well, we're caught. I would have had you if not for that landing. But I guess I'm just unlucky."

I was smiling away when he cunningly sneaked a hand behind himself and threw a knife at me. The knife went through my shoulder, pinning me down to the mast. I cried out in pain and, firing both pistols in shock, I dropped them into the water. And along with them, Israel Hands, too, fell into the sea.

As Israel sank into the water, I saw the surface turning red with his blood. I could not loosen the dagger and yet I was afraid I would fall to my death beside Israel. That thought was enough to help me pull myself loose from the mast. I was only pinned by the tiniest piece of my shoulder, mostly by my shirt. I slowly crawled down the mast and then, looking around, decided to throw the other dead man off the ship. I left the ship after setting her straight.

I leaped off the deck and happily headed for the forest. As darkness fell, I was confused about the direction. Soon, my path was lit by the moonlight. When I came to the stockade, I saw the smoldering remains of fire. I stood there wondering why there had been such a huge fire.

I immediately thought that something had gone amiss while I was away, so I began to crawl on

my hands and knees. When I got to the door and stood up, I could see absolutely nothing. I walked in and thought of going to sleep in my corner, surprising them in the morning. Just then I heard a shrill cry, one that chilled my heart. "Pieces of eight! Pieces of eight!" the voice kept repeating.

It was Long John Silver's parrot, Captain Flint! He was the watch, and he had found me. I turned to hear Long John's voice saying, "Who goes there?"

I turned, only to run into dead bodies lying all around.

"Dick! Get some light here!" cried Long John, when I was caught. A man left and soon came back with a flaming torch.

Chapter 21

In the Enemy's Camp

In the red glow of the torch, I knew all was lost. Six pirates had taken over the stockade. I could only assume that my friends were killed. The parrot sat on Long John's shoulder.

"Well!" he said. "If it isn't young Jim Hawkins! "Well, I was always keen on you joining us. It seems your friends don't want you anymore since you deserted them again." When he said that, I knew that my friends were alive.

"Your friends woke up to see the ship gone and came to us to make terms. We took the stockade, and they took leave."

"Well, I was the one who ruined your mutiny. I killed Israel

Hands and cut the ship's cable and hid it where you'll never find it. Go ahead, kill me. If you keep me alive, I will testify against you in court," I replied bravely.

When the other pirates got upset, Long John told them off by saying that I was braver than any one of them. On this, one of the men came forward and asked if they could hold a council, but

without Long John Silver as a part of it. When he agreed, they went outside, leaving me alone with him. When he looked at me, his eyes held fear.

"They'll turn against me, Jim. We must save each other! I know you have a ship somewhere. Now, you tell me, why would the doctor give me the map to the treasure before he left?" I stood there with my mouth open in shock.

When the mutineers returned, Long John looked friendly again. But the men entered slowly, looking desperate and mean, and Long John knew what was up.

"Give it to me already!" he barked, and sure enough, they handed him the Black Spot.

He read what was written: "Deposed," which meant that he was no longer captain. One man, George Merry, told him the charges.

John said, "How dare you accuse me and try to be captain over me! You do not know of our sticky situation. As for the boy, he's our hostage. How can I kill our only hostage? He could be our last chance. You would have made the same deal I have, part of which was the doctor coming every day to see to your wounds. What's more, I've got something that will tell you why!"

He dropped the map on the floor. Seeing this, the pirates fell on it like dogs on a bone. When the men chanted, "Captain Silver, Captain Silver," George remained quiet. Long John looked at him. "Well, it looks like you'll have to wait for your turn."

Chapter 22

Jim and the Treasure Hunt

We woke up when the doctor arrived, and I was ashamed to even look at him. Long John Silver was bright and merry. "Good morning Doctor! Come and see, your patients are all doing well." While

the doctor made his way up the hill, Long John added, "And there is a little stranger who would like to meet you." The doctor stopped right there. "Jim?" he said. "But, of course!" said Long John.

Shocked as he was, the doctor decided to talk to me after he was done with his patients. After attending to their wounds, he

asked to speak to me alone, to which the men objected.

"Silence!" roared Long John. He turned to the doctor. "Now, sir, we are very grateful for your help. Hawkins, do you promise not to run away?" I did. Long John then asked the doctor to take a walk down the hill and that he would walk me out.

Once outside the door, his behavior changed completely. He looked at the doctor, "Now, Doctor, I've saved Jim's life and I am only here now to save mine. I hope you will help me."

"Aren't you afraid?" asked the doctor.

"Very," admitted John. "I will be hanged, for sure. But I hope that you will know that I did some good in saving Jim's life."

With that, Long John left. The doctor scolded me until he heard my story. "You've found the ship? You've been the one saving us all along!"

He encouraged me to break my word and come with him, but I didn't do so. I had given an oath.

Once back with Long John, the doctor told him it was best not to find the treasure.

"I have to, or else they'll kill me themselves," replied Long John.

The doctor said, "Then I warn you to beware of the high winds at sea. Those waves can kill. If we get out of this alive, I promise to do

everything in my power to save you."

Long John beamed and thanked the doctor. The doctor then shook my hand and left.

Long John Silver then turned to me and said, "If I've saved your life, you've saved mine. I saw how the doctor asked you to run. By not doing so, you saved my life. I suggest we stick together for the hunt."

We had our breakfast after that, where Long John's manner changed again. He became really loud and boastful.

I was worried I'd miss the reasons behind my friends' doings. Why did they leave the fort and give up the map? What was the warning of the waves about? All these doubts filled my head when we left for the treasure hunt.

Each of the pirates was armed with several weapons; Long John led the party with two rifles; pistols; a cutlass; and Captain Flint jabbering away. Along the way, the men looked at the chart and argued over which tall tree the mark might be. Each picked his favorite. We walked and turned left, walking up a crest. The jungle

became dense. Just then, we heard one of the men cry out. We ran to him and saw him staring at the skeleton of a man by a tree. The skeleton was laid out straight, which was odd.

"This is our pointer," said Long John. "This is one of Flint's jokes. Let's move."

The men walked more closely and silently. The skeleton had made all their spirits drop.

Chapter 23

The Fright and the Treasure

The men were exhausted and sat down at first chance. They began to talk to about Pirate Flint.

"He was ugly. And he had a violent temper."

"You should be glad he's dead then," said Long John. Just then, we all heard a voice call out:

"Fifteen men on a dead man's chest—
Yo-Ho-Ho and a bottle of rum!"

"It's Flint! He's back from the dead!" cried the mutineers.

"Fetch me my sword, Darby!" the voice called out again.

"Those were his last words!" said one of the men there.

The pirates stood rooted to the spot, each one crying out that they were afraid of ghosts. One man

read from his Bible. Long John lashed out, "That was an echo! Ghosts don't have echoes! That's a living being."

This seemed to bring the men to their senses. "Yes. That didn't sound like Flint. It sounded like Ben Gunn!"

Obviously, no one feared Ben Gunn, even if they thought him dead. The men were back on track and focused on the climb ahead. Long John pulled me by the rope by which he had tied my hand. His mood had changed. I could see that the treasure was all he was focusing on. There was no mercy left in him. He would find the treasure and kill anyone who came in his way.

Just then, we entered a clearing and heard George cry out. We ran to him and saw before us a great hole; we could tell it was not freshly dug. Grass had grown on the caved-in sides. At the bottom were bits of packing crates from Flint's ship, the *Walrus*. But we all realized one thing: The loot had been found, and 700 pounds of treasure were gone!

The men jumped into the pit to find one single coin. They climbed out and threw murderous glances toward Long John. George cried out, "This wooden-legged fool got us here. Look at him! He knew all along there was no treasure!"

Long John spoke up. "Back to seeking the post of Captain, George?"

They stood across us and we looked toward them, our pistols ready.

"What are the odds? One cripple and a boy against five of us," said George.

Just then, shots rang out and two of the men were hit—George fell into the pit. The doctor, Gray, and Ben joined us with smoking pistols. We ran quickly through the woods to cut off those men escaping. We found out that they went the wrong way.

Ben, in his yearlong wanderings, had found the skeleton and the treasure. He had dug up the gold and moved it to his cave two months before we had come to the island.

We made our way to the boats and paddled by the mouth of Ben's cave, where we saw the squire waving to us. We also saw the *Hispaniola* floating offshore. We entered the cove and saw Captain Smollett lying beside a fire, and also great heaps of gold and treasure. I thought of the many who had died trying to find and claim it.

"Never again to sea—eh, Jim?" asked the doctor.

Chapter 24

And Last

The next few days were spent taking the treasure to the *Hispaniola.* By every evening a fortune had been stowed aboard, and there was more fortune waiting to be stowed the next day!

We loaded Ben's cave with a good stock of food and supplies. As we were leaving, we passed the surviving mutineers. They begged

us to take them along. but we decided not to do so.

I felt extreme joy in leaving Treasure Island. Long John took a small craft and a sack of treasure and made off. We were relieved to see that he was gone. We heard no more of him. I believe he built a new life for himself and was still living with his parrot.

When we eventually got home, we all went our separate ways, each with a share of the treasure.

About the Author

Robert Louis Stevenson was a Scottish novelist, poet, and travel writer. He was greatly admired by other authors. He was popular. He studied to become a lawyer, but he never practiced law.

He traveled often in search of better climates for his health. However, at the age of forty-four, he died of tuberculosis. He was born on November 13, 1850, and died on December 3, 1894.

Treasure Island was his first major success. It was a tale of piracy, buried treasure, and adventure. Originally, this story was called *The Sea Cook*.